GAME ON IN
ANCIENT
GREECE

GAME? Are you kidding me?

This is going to hurt. This is really going to hurt.

Written by **Linda Bailey**

Illustrated by **Bill Slavin**

D1248347

Kids Can Press

This book is for my friend and writing colleague, Deborah Hodge, with thanks for her insight and advice, lo these many books — L.B.

For Graham, the God of Agility — B.S.

Acknowledgments

We are extremely grateful to Dr. Mark Golden of the University of Winnipeg for his thoughtful review of the manuscript and art, and for his generosity with time and advice. Thanks also to Dr. M. Eleanor Irwin of the University of Toronto, who reviewed an earlier version.

Game On in Ancient Greece has involved the efforts of many, and we want to thank the wonderful team at Kids Can Press who helped bring this book to life, especially Valerie Wyatt, Julia Naimska, Genie MacLeod, Yvette Ghione and Katie Gray.

And finally, thanks again to the book's first readers: Nico Lauck Stephenson, Jeremie Lauck Stephenson, Dylan Maxwell and Ian McLellan.

Kids Can Press gratefully acknowledges the financial support of the Government of Ontario, through Ontario Creates; the Ontario Arts Council; the Canada Council for the Arts; and the Government of Canada for our publishing activity.

Published in Canada and the U.S. by Kids Can Press Ltd.
25 Dockside Drive, Toronto, ON M5A 0B5

Kids Can Press is a Corus Entertainment Inc. company

www.kidscanpress.com

The artwork in this book was rendered in pen and ink and watercolor.
The text is set in Adobe Jenson Pro and Rainier.

Edited by Valerie Wyatt
Designed by Julia Naimska

Printed and bound in Buji, Shenzhen, China, in 3/2019 by WKT Company
CM 19 0 9 8 7 6 5 4 3 2 1
CM PA 19 0 9 8 7 6 5 4 3 2 1

Library and Archives Canada Cataloguing in Publication

Bailey, Linda, 1948–
[Adventures in ancient Greece]
Game on in ancient Greece / written by Linda Bailey ; illustrated by Bill Slavin.

(The time travel guides ; 4)
Previously published under title: Adventures in ancient Greece. Toronto: Kids Can Press, 2002.
Includes index.
ISBN 978-1-77138-988-4 (softcover). ISBN 978-1-5253-0273-2 (hardcover)

1. Greece — History — To 146 B.C — Comic books, strips, etc. 2. Greece — History — To 146 B.C — Juvenile literature. 3. Greece — Civilization — To 146 B.C — Comic books, strips, etc. 4. Greece — Civilization — To 146 B.C — Juvenile literature. 5. Olympic games (Ancient — Comic books, strips, etc. 6. Olympic games (Ancient — Juvenile literature. 7. Nonfiction comics. 8. Comics (Graphic works). I. Slavin, Bill, illustrator II. Title. III. Title: Adventures in ancient Greece.

DF77.B26 2019   j938   C2018-905841-2

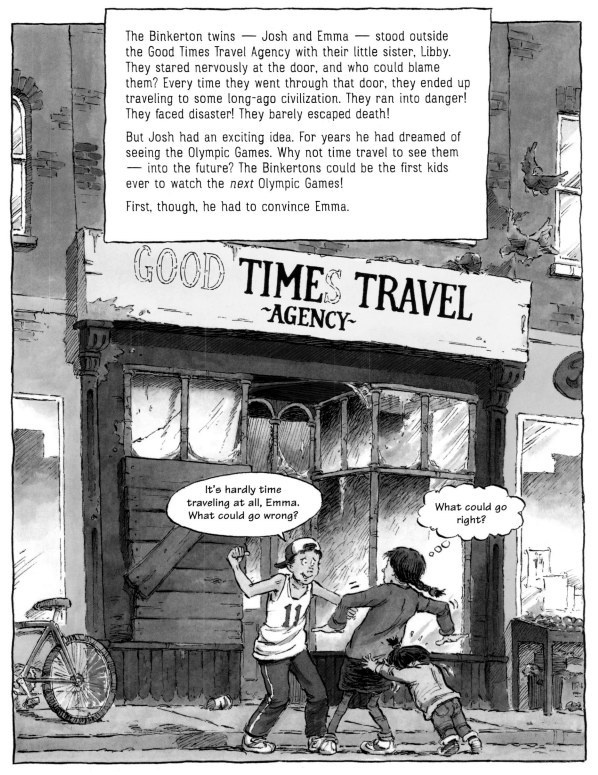

The Binkerton twins — Josh and Emma — stood outside the Good Times Travel Agency with their little sister, Libby. They stared nervously at the door, and who could blame them? Every time they went through that door, they ended up traveling to some long-ago civilization. They ran into danger! They faced disaster! They barely escaped death!

But Josh had an exciting idea. For years he had dreamed of seeing the Olympic Games. Why not time travel to see them — into the future? The Binkertons could be the first kids ever to watch the *next* Olympic Games!

First, though, he had to convince Emma.

Emma couldn't hold out forever. Before she knew it, she was through the door, inside the agency — and under the nose of Julian T. Pettigrew, the owner.

Customers?
Come in, come in.
No time like the present.

You can say that again.

5

Josh worked up his courage and told Mr. Pettigrew why they'd come.

Eh?

We want to go forward in time, sir — to the next Olympic Games.

Josh did his best to explain ... but it was hard to compete with Libby.

Sports? Every four years? The Olympic Ga—

LIBBY!

Mr. Pettigrew must have gotten the message because he headed for his bookcase of travel guidebooks.

Olympic Games ... hmmmm.

You promised to behave this time, Libby.

I will.

Josh and Emma were so rattled by Libby's behavior, they didn't bother to look closely at the title of the Guidebook. This was a mistake. A *big* mistake!

Julian T. Pettigrew's Personal Guide to ANCIENT GREECE

Open this book and your journey's begun.
Read every word and your journey is done.

With a shiver of excitement, Josh flung the book open. There was a terrible, wonderful flash and ...

... the Binkertons were there!

But where, exactly, was there?

This didn't look *anything* like the Olympic Games they'd seen on TV! They quickly checked the Guidebook.

This is a battlefield! What are we doing here?

I don't belieeeve it! We're in ancient Greece — where the Olympics first began!

JULIAN T. PETTIGREW'S PERSONAL GUIDE TO ANCIENT GREECE

WELCOME to ancient Greece — an excellent holiday choice.

But what terrible timing! You seem to have arrived right in the middle of a battle.

Unfortunately, battles happen here all the time. Greece in the fifth century BCE is made up of several hundred city-states (cities plus the countryside around them). These city-states don't always get along. Mostly they fight over farmland, which is scarce in Greece because of all the mountains.

The foot soldiers in a Greek battle are called hoplites. They wear armor made of bronze or reinforced layers of stiff linen, and their fighting style is simple. They pack themselves together, eight rows deep, in a formation called a phalanx. When the bugle sounds, they jog forward together.

Sticking together is important! Each hoplite carries a shield called a hoplon. And as long as the hoplites fight shoulder-to-shoulder, most of them will be protected by their neighbors' shields as well as their own.

Eventually, the two sides come together with a mighty crash! The front soldiers start jabbing the enemy with their spears. The back soldiers try to push the front soldiers forward, through the enemy line. War cries fill the air! Swords come out! It's brutal, it's ferocious, and the very worst spot is in the middle!

If you're watching a battle, be careful — and whatever you do, don't *ever* get stuck between two lines of hoplites.

9

But there was no time to talk. The battle lines were getting closer. The Binkertons were about to become the filling in a soldier sandwich! Frantically, they searched for cover.

I hate it when this happens.

This is going to hurt. This is really going to hurt.

The Binkertons waited to be crushed like walnuts between the two opposing armies. But minutes passed ... and nothing happened.

I think they're leaving.

City-States — Separate, but Still Greek

Greece is a land of steep mountains and lonely islands, so the city-states are mostly cut off from one another. No wonder they don't get along!

Each city-state is like a tiny separate country. It has the same language, religion, beliefs and general customs as its neighbors, but it's not united with them in any way. Most people are fiercely loyal to their own city-state. They're ready

Athens and Sparta are the two main city-states.

A man wearing a wreath on his head seemed to be the center of attention. Creeping closer, the Binkertons discovered that he was announcing a truce.

I love this guy!

You must cease your fighting until the Olympic Games are over.

All Emma felt was relief. The truce would give them enough time to read the Guidebook so they could go home.

But Josh was still eager to see some Olympic Games. He didn't even mind if they were ancient!

It's a once-in-a-lifetime opportunity.

I just want to have a lifetime.

to defend it — to the death if necessary. Still, the people who live in city-states *are* all Greeks. From time to time, they get together at all-Greek festivals where they honor their gods by competing in sporting contests. One of these festivals is the Olympic Games, which take place every four years.

When it's time for the Olympic Games, the Greek city-states put aside their quarrels. Truce-bearers travel all over the Greek world to tell people the date of the festival and to announce that wars must stop. Anyone who wants to travel to the Games can do so without fear. This time of peace is called the Olympic truce.

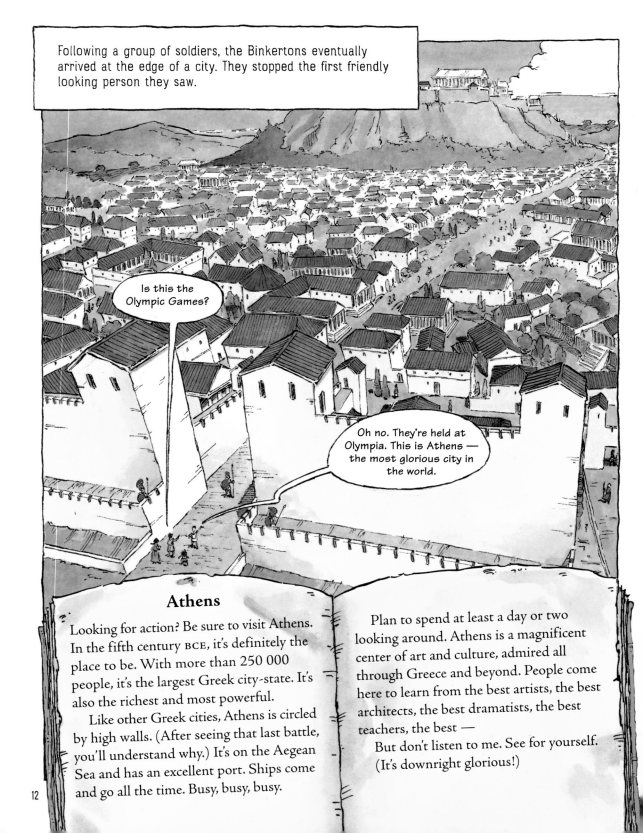

Following a group of soldiers, the Binkertons eventually arrived at the edge of a city. They stopped the first friendly looking person they saw.

Is this the Olympic Games?

Oh no. They're held at Olympia. This is Athens — the most glorious city in the world.

Athens

Looking for action? Be sure to visit Athens. In the fifth century BCE, it's definitely the place to be. With more than 250 000 people, it's the largest Greek city-state. It's also the richest and most powerful.

Like other Greek cities, Athens is circled by high walls. (After seeing that last battle, you'll understand why.) It's on the Aegean Sea and has an excellent port. Ships come and go all the time. Busy, busy, busy.

Plan to spend at least a day or two looking around. Athens is a magnificent center of art and culture, admired all through Greece and beyond. People come here to learn from the best artists, the best architects, the best dramatists, the best teachers, the best —
But don't listen to me. See for yourself. (It's downright glorious!)

The boy, whose name was Demeas, promised to help the Binkertons get to the Olympics. First, though, he insisted on showing them around Athens — starting with a hill called the Pnyx.

Emma listened politely. But Josh had a one-track mind — and guess who was on the track?

It doesn't look like much now, but when there's an assembly, thousands of men come here to vote.

Men? Just men?

YAY, JOSH!

BRAVO! AMAZING!

Democracy in Athens

Are you at the Pnyx yet? Pay close attention. History is being made here!

Greece is the first place where ordinary people get to rule their own country. The ancient Greeks call this kind of government "demokratia" ("demos" means people, and "kratos" means power). Later in history, it will be called "democracy."

Here's how it works. There's no king here. No president or prime minister either. Instead, ordinary citizens have a huge meeting every nine or ten days on the Pnyx to vote on things of concern. It's called the Assembly.

Anyone can speak. The audience laughs, hisses, boos or claps for the speakers. Then they vote by raising their hands.

But wait a minute! Not *everyone* gets to vote. You have to be male, free (not a slave) and born to Athenian parents. This means no women can vote. Neither can the thousands of slaves, or people who have come here from other places.

Well, okay, democracy here isn't perfect. But it *is* an important contribution of the ancient Greeks. Democracy will grow and spread all over the world.

13

Demeas loved his city and was a very enthusiastic tour guide. This would have been terrific — if the Binkertons had *wanted* a tour guide.

The next thing they knew, they were at a theater where a play was being rehearsed.

Isn't it magnificent?

Sure. Great. Magnificent. Can we go to the Olympics now?

Libby? Where's —? LIBBY! You get OUT of there.

Greek Theater

Here's another "first" for the ancient Greeks — the world's first theaters! Don't expect a movie, though. Greek theaters show live performances of plays. They're built outdoors on hillsides and have seats for up to 14 000 people, packed in like sardines.

Try to get a seat near the front. But if you end up in the back row, don't worry. Greek theaters are built so that sound will carry, even without microphones (which won't be invented for another few thousand years).

Greek plays may look a little strange to you. For one thing, there are usually no more than three main actors. Each actor may play several roles, wearing different masks. There's also a group of guys called the chorus who sing, dance and speak to the audience.

Guys? Did I say "guys"? Greek theater has only male actors — even for the female roles. (Sorry, girls.)

Josh was more than ready to leave Athens, but Demeas wouldn't hear of it! Promising his new friends a delicious treat, he hurried them along to the marketplace.

Olives! The best in the world.

This is a treat?

I think I'll ... er ... save mine for later.

The Agora

Would you like to buy some flowers? Fish? Fruit? Firewood? Footwear? Come to the marketplace! It's called the agora, and you can buy (or sell) almost anything here.

But the agora isn't just a market. It's also a meeting place and the heart of any Greek city. People get together with friends here and chat about business or government — or just share the latest gossip. Pick a shady spot under one of the stoas (long open buildings with columns) and start talking. The Athenians are great talkers.

If you have extra cash, bring it along. There are bankers and moneylenders who would love to meet you and your Athenian money (silver coins with owls stamped on them). Don't have a wallet? Try carrying your money ancient Greek style — in your mouth.

Blech!

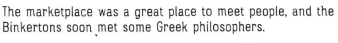

The marketplace was a great place to meet people, and the Binkertons soon met some Greek philosophers.

They were very interesting. (Well, not really.)

What is justice?

What should human beings aim for?

What do we mean when we say that something exists?

What do I have to do to get to the Olympics?

Greek Philosophers

Thinking of leaving Athens? Think again. Think hard!

You won't be the only one thinking in ancient Greece. People here love to think — and to discuss what they're thinking about. The ancient Greeks are a curious bunch, eager to know about the world and how it works. Some think about the stars and nature. Others think about mathematical problems. Still others think about people and how they should behave. Some try to answer difficult questions such as "What is beauty?" and "What is love?"

These ancient Greek thinkers are called philosophers ("lovers of wisdom"). They like to travel around, teaching their ideas to others. Watch for them in the agora, sitting around in small groups, arguing and discussing … and thinking, of course. If you're in a thoughtful mood, join in. Or maybe you'd rather just listen and …

Hey! YOU! Wake up! PAY ATTENTION!

The ideas of the most famous Greek philosophers (Socrates, Plato, Aristotle) are important. They will last for a very long time, so LISTEN UP!

Emma noticed that she wasn't seeing many women in Athens.

Most of them are at home.

Doing what?

CLAP! CLAP!

When she spotted some girls at a fountain, she stopped to say hello.

Why aren't you at home?

We're slaves. We have work to do!

Seeing how heavy their jars were, Emma offered to help.

No, wait! I can do it!

But there are times when being helpful just isn't very ... helpful.

You wouldn't happen to have a tube of Wonder Glue? Er, no, I guess not.

Greek Society

Who's who in ancient Athens?

Basically, there are two groups: male citizens who get to vote and ... everyone else (women, slaves and foreigners)!

Women generally marry young (at 14 or 15). Wealthy women spend most of their time at home, running their households. When they go out, it's for funerals and religious festivals, or to visit. Poor women *have* to go out — to fetch water, to work or to trade at the market.

Athenian families generally have at least one or two slaves who do most of the household work. Well-educated slaves might tutor the family's children. Slaves also work in the family business or on the family farm. Some slaves come from outside Greece, captured by slave traders. Others are the children of slaves.

Finally, there are the metics — people who have come to live in Athens from elsewhere. Some run businesses and are quite rich. Metics can never be citizens. Like women and slaves, they will never be able to vote.

(Neither can you, no matter how long you stay here. Forget it.)

17

Emma did her best to enjoy herself in Athens ...

And most glorious of all is — the Parthenon!

Oh, my! It really is glorious.

Very nice. Now what about those Games?

... but she was definitely having a bad day. Maybe even a bad century! When some Greek garbage got tossed, she was right in its path.

Not ... having ... fun.

Marvelous!

Can I drive?

The Parthenon

Look up. Look way up. That rocky hill overlooking the city is called the Acropolis. To the Athenians, it's a sacred area. That large building on top, made of creamy white marble, is called the Parthenon. It was built to honor Athena, goddess of Athens.

Take a close look at the Parthenon's columns. They appear to be straight, right? Guess what? They're not. Straight columns would look saggy from a distance. In order to make the Parthenon's columns *look* straight, the builders made them bulge in the middle. It's an optical illusion!

Inside the Parthenon is a huge statue of Athena covered with ivory and gold. Outside is an even larger bronze Athena, holding a gold-tipped spear. She's like a beacon to sailors, who can see her from far out at sea.

Things went from bad to worse when Demeas invited the Binkertons home. They were barely through the door when Emma and Libby got whisked away.

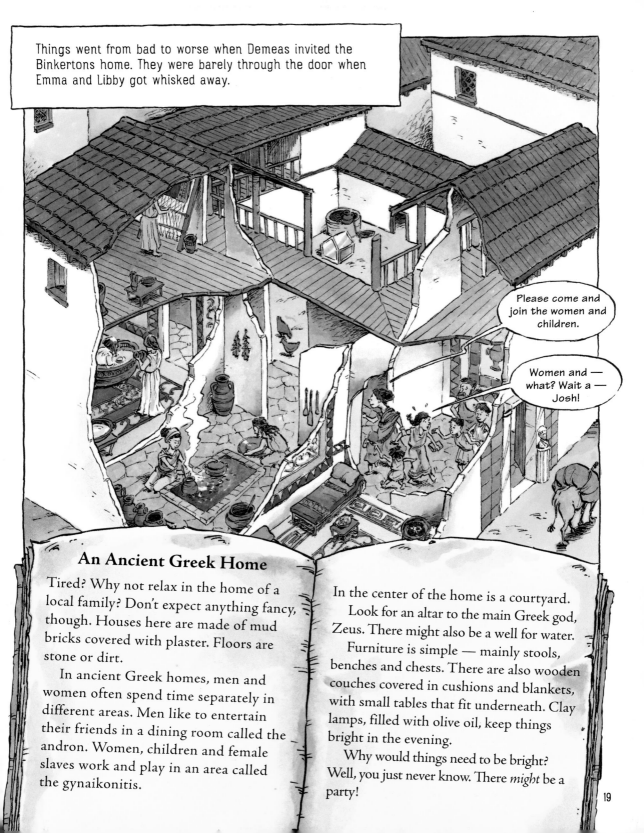

Please come and join the women and children.

Women and — what? Wait a — Josh!

An Ancient Greek Home

Tired? Why not relax in the home of a local family? Don't expect anything fancy, though. Houses here are made of mud bricks covered with plaster. Floors are stone or dirt.

In ancient Greek homes, men and women often spend time separately in different areas. Men like to entertain their friends in a dining room called the andron. Women, children and female slaves work and play in an area called the gynaikonitis.

In the center of the home is a courtyard.

Look for an altar to the main Greek god, Zeus. There might also be a well for water.

Furniture is simple — mainly stools, benches and chests. There are also wooden couches covered in cushions and blankets, with small tables that fit underneath. Clay lamps, filled with olive oil, keep things bright in the evening.

Why would things need to be bright? Well, you just never know. There *might* be a party!

That evening, there was a dinner party at Demeas's house, with plenty of food, drink and entertainment. Emma enjoyed the music … from a distance.

But Josh got a close-up look.

Food & Dinner Parties

Hungry? Lie down and have something to eat! Ancient Greek food is simple and healthy — bread or porridge (made from barley or wheat), fruit, vegetables and cheese. Most Greeks also enjoy seafood, eggs and poultry — and all the olives they can eat.

Meat is eaten mostly on special occasions, such as festivals and weddings. Try an olive, instead. Don't like olives? Oh, dear. Greece is serious olive-growing country. You'd better *start* liking them.

The ancient Greeks often have dinner parties called symposia. (Sorry, they're only for men.)

Guests at a symposium take off their sandals and lie on couches to eat. They wear garlands on their heads and are waited on by slaves.

What do you do at a symposium? You eat, of course. (There'll be plenty of olives.) For drinks, there's wine mixed with water. Sometimes there are entertainers. Other times, guests provide their own entertainment — singing, reciting poetry, asking riddles or playing games. Here's a game for you! Wait till your cup is almost empty and then flick what's left at a target. It's called kottabos.

First thing next morning, the Binkertons cornered Demeas and demanded his help to get to Olympia. It turned out he was traveling there himself, on his uncle's boat.

He invited Josh along — but not the girls.

That did it! Now Emma was determined to go to the Olympic Games, even if she had to walk every step of the way.

Olympia turned out to be a long, long, *long* walk away. The road was rough and hilly.

Hasn't anyone here ever heard of a bus?

There had to be an easier way. Josh thought he'd found it when he met a group of travelers from Sparta.

They have horses — and carts! Come on!

Carts? Can I drive?

Getting around in Ancient Greece

Need to travel in ancient Greece? Here's a word of advice. Water!

Traveling by sea is by far the best way to go. On a ship, you can easily "hop" from island to island … and let the wind do the work. And bonus — the sea is flat! No need to climb hills.

If you have to go by land, too bad.

There are few roads in this mountainous country, and those that exist are steep, rocky and full of ruts. When the Olympic Games are on, the roads are crowded, too. Try to get a hold of a mule or a donkey to carry your belongings. Maybe a passing ox-cart will give you a lift.

Chances are, though, you'll have to walk. (Have an olive. It will cheer you up.)

23

The Binkertons soon discovered that the *last* place you should look for an easy life is among a group of Spartans.

Sparta and the Spartans

The Athenians are interesting, but if you really want an adventure, get to know some Spartans!

Sparta is a powerful Greek city-state that is quite different from the others. For one thing, all Spartan men are professional soldiers. They spend all their time fighting and training for war. (The citizens of other city-states work as farmers or craftsmen and only fight part-time.)

It's not easy being raised a Spartan. When you're born, the elders check you over. If you look weak or sick, you may be left on a nearby mountain to die. If you're a boy, you'll be taken from your mother at about age seven to live in army barracks and train as a soldier.

You'll be expected to put up with cold, pain and hunger and become a tough Spartan warrior. You'll go barefoot and have to eat black broth — a horrible soup made of pork, pig's blood and vinegar. It's famous all over Greece for its nastiness.

Don't expect your mother to help you. Spartan women are raised to be strong and to produce tough warrior sons. Your mother will send you off to war, telling you to come home *with* your shield (a brave soldier) or *on* your shield (a dead soldier!). If you're cowardly and lose your shield, don't come home at all. There are stories of Spartan mothers killing their sons for cowardice.

Leaving the Spartans behind, the Binkertons straggled on alone. But as they got close to Olympia, Josh began to worry. What if Emma and Libby weren't allowed to watch the Games?

Don't worry. I've got it all figured out.

Remember what Demeas said?

It wasn't hard to make Libby look like a boy ...

What do you think?

Even her own brother couldn't tell.

Ancient Greek Clothing & Hairstyles

Man, woman or child — in ancient Greece, you'll wear a chiton. It's a simple rectangle of wool or linen cloth fastened at the shoulders and sides, leaving gaps for your head and arms. A soft belt around your waist finishes it off. Women wear their chitons ankle-length, but slaves, children and working men wear them shorter, to the knees. In cool weather, you can also wear a himation (cloak) over your chiton. Add a pair of sandals, and — presto! — you're a well-dressed ancient Greek.

Hairstyles are more complicated. Men generally have short hair and beards, while boys grow their hair long — except in Sparta, where boys have short hair and men have long hair. Women and girls wear their hair very long. Before marriage, they wear it in ringlets. After marriage, they pile it up on top of their heads with ribbons, pins and decorations.

See what I mean? Hair is complicated. But don't worry about it. Just try to stay cool. Summers in Greece can get very, very hot. Aren't you glad your clothes are loose and light?

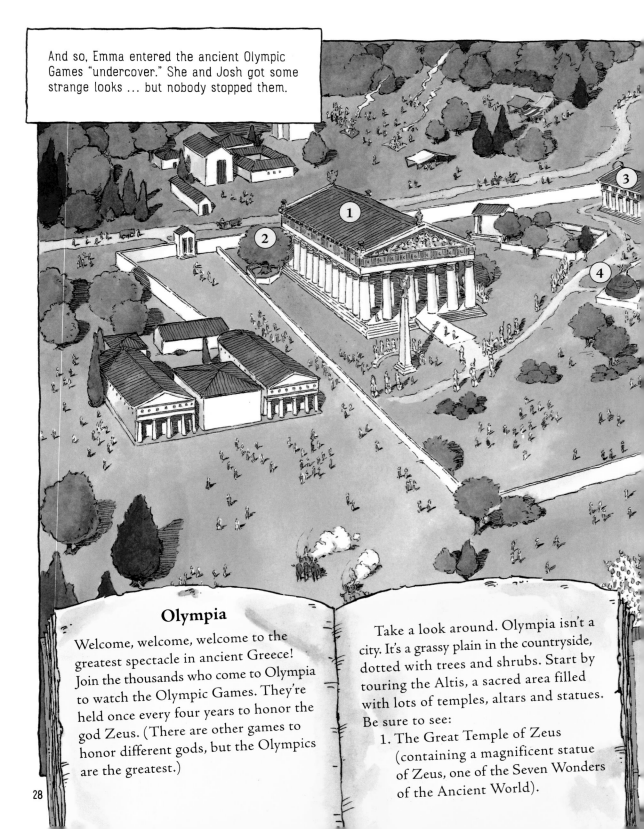

And so, Emma entered the ancient Olympic Games "undercover." She and Josh got some strange looks ... but nobody stopped them.

Olympia

Welcome, welcome, welcome to the greatest spectacle in ancient Greece! Join the thousands who come to Olympia to watch the Olympic Games. They're held once every four years to honor the god Zeus. (There are other games to honor different gods, but the Olympics are the greatest.)

Take a look around. Olympia isn't a city. It's a grassy plain in the countryside, dotted with trees and shrubs. Start by touring the Altis, a sacred area filled with lots of temples, altars and statues. Be sure to see:
1. The Great Temple of Zeus (containing a magnificent statue of Zeus, one of the Seven Wonders of the Ancient World).

Such long legs! Will you be running in the Games?

Er ... only if I have to.

Air ... give me air ...

Hey, guys! Good to see you. Great games, eh?

Getting really hot in here.

2. The sacred olive tree, from which winners' wreaths are cut by a boy with a golden sickle.

3. The Temple of Hera, Zeus's wife.

4. The Great Altar of Zeus.

When you're done here, look for the Stadium (running track for foot races) and the Hippodrome (horse track). Get to these tracks early to see the races!

And now for the bad news. Do not expect to be comfortable while you're here. It's midsummer and scorching hot. There are flies everywhere. It's crowded, dusty and noisy. There's nowhere to wash and hardly anywhere to sleep (except outside). The drinking water is likely stagnant, and you'll probably *never* find a toilet.

Aside from all that ... it's a very nice place. Enjoy!

When the Binkertons sat down to watch the Games, they got a big surprise.

Down in front!

I can't see!

Can I look now?

I'm not sure you'll want to.

The Olympic Games

Don't just stand there, gaping. Find a place to sit. Forty thousand people are competing with you for the best viewing spot, so hurry!

Settled? Good. If you're wearing a hat, take it off. Hats block people's views and are forbidden here.

As you watch these ancient Games, you'll probably notice some differences

from the modern Olympics. For instance:

+ No team sports.
+ No water sports.
+ No clothes!

No clothes for the athletes, anyway. In the ancient Olympic Games, they compete naked. One explanation is that long ago an athlete's clothing fell off during a race. When he won, he started a new fashion.

But clothing or not, the Games were definitely exciting! In fact, they were so exciting that the Binkertons soon forgot the athletes' (missing) uniforms.

Following the crowds from event to event, they watched as much as they could.

WRESTLING

RUNNING

BOXING

PENTATHLON

PANKRATION

Do your best to see the main events while you are here. Aside from the equestrian (horse) sports, they are:

- Running — a short sprint, a longer sprint and a long race
- Wrestling — a contest requiring skill and grace
- Boxing — a match between boxers wearing leather strips around their hands
- Pentathlon — a five-sport event that includes running, long jump, wrestling, javelin-throwing and discus-throwing
- Pankration — a vicious combination of wrestling and boxing

If you don't like violence, stay away from the pankration. Competitors are allowed to punch, hit, wrestle, twist arms, break fingers, even strangle their opponents. Some pankratiasts actually lose their lives!

There are also separate events for boys 12 to 18 and a race in armor for hoplite soldiers who clank and clatter down the track.

And the grand prize for the winner of any Olympic event is … a wreath of olive branches! (Doesn't sound like much? Don't worry. Winners are very well treated by their city-states when they go home.)

33

In the end, Josh and Emma got so interested in the Games that they stopped paying attention to their little sister.

This was a big mistake.

It's the chariot races!

Libby? Where's Libby?

Equestrian Events

Ready for a wild ride? Hurry down to the Hippodrome (horse track) to see the equestrian (horse) events.

The horse races are a big thrill here at the ancient Olympics. Saddles and stirrups haven't yet been invented, so the jockeys ride bareback with their feet hanging loose. Is it hard to hang on? Is it hard to control the horse? You bet!

The chariot races are even more exciting — and dangerous. There are two kinds of races — two-horse and four-horse. It's a rough, tooth-jarring ride. The Hippodrome isn't circular like a modern racetrack. It's a straight track, so the chariots have to go back and forth, turning around a post at each end.

That's where it gets really dangerous — at the posts. If, by some chance, you end up driving a chariot (a very bad idea, by the way), TRY TO STAY AHEAD ON THE TURNS! Terrible things can happen if you don't. Your wheels could lock! Your chariot might flip! You could smash into other chariots — or the post! Even if you don't crash, it will be *chaos* out there, with shouting drivers, straining horses, clouds of dust and nasty pileups.

No wonder this is the most dangerous event in the whole ancient Olympics! (It's also one of the most popular.)

Libby managed to hang on for two laps. She even took the lead! But, like many charioteers, she had a little trouble on the turns.

LIB-BEEEEE!

Josh and Emma ran as quickly as possible —
not very quickly, of course — to the middle
of the Hippodrome. By the time they got
there, Libby was gone.

Have you seen a little
gir ... er, boy ... about
this big?

Josh and Emma would have been desperate
with worry if they hadn't known their sister
so well.

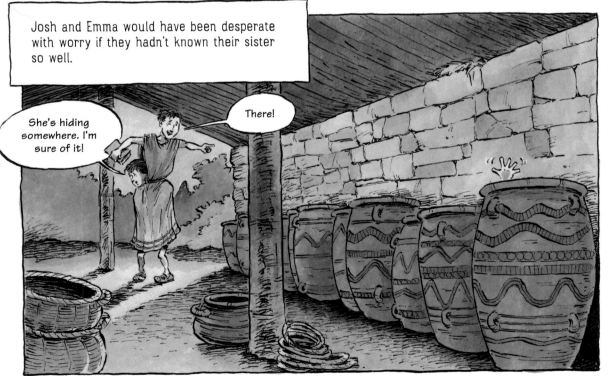

She's hiding
somewhere. I'm
sure of it!

There!

Libby was now the least popular person in all of Olympia. Josh and Emma realized that they would have to sneak her out. There was only one way.

Are you sure this will work?

No problem!

Big problem!

Trying to find their way out of Olympia, the Binkertons got caught up in a huge crowd. It carried them toward a tall altar — and what looked like the biggest barbecue Josh had ever seen!

Holy smoke!

Exactly!

With Libby hidden under his chiton, Josh was not only tall; he was also lumpy.

Shouldn't have eaten all those olives.

Greek Religion & Sacrifices

With so many sports going on, it's easy to forget that the Olympic Games are first of all a religious festival. They're held to honor the god Zeus, whom the Greeks believe to be ruler of the world.

The ancient Greeks have many gods. The twelve most important are believed to live on Mount Olympus, the highest mountain in Greece. They include Zeus (god of the sky and weather), Poseidon (ruler of the seas), Hera (goddess of women and marriage), and Aphrodite (goddess of love). The ancient Greeks believe that these gods have power over their lives and can help or harm them. To keep the gods happy, people offer prayers and sacrifices. They also hold festivals (such as the Olympic Games).

During the Olympic Games, there is a great sacrifice to Zeus. A hundred oxen are slaughtered, and their thigh bones are burned on an altar as a gift to Zeus, who is thought to enjoy the smoke. The rest of the oxen meat is roasted and eaten by spectators. Stick around and look hungry — there may be a spare rib for you. (Believe me, Zeus will never miss it.)

The Binkertons hadn't had much to eat during the Games, so they hung around. When the barbecued meat was handed out, Josh quickly made up for lost time.

His sisters weren't so lucky.

Hey! What's that smell?

Joshy? Are you eating?

It took a few pinches from his sisters, but Josh did find a way to share.

Oops! Dropped it. What a butterfingers! Could I have another, please?

The Greeks were definitely getting suspicious. Still, it might have been all right except for ...

Libby!

?!

Gimme that!

The Binkertons' secret was out —

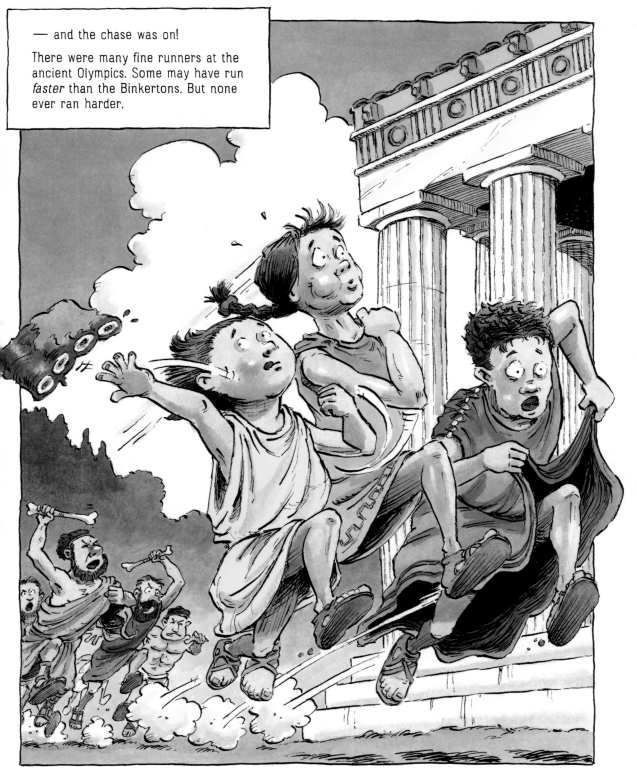

— and the chase was on!

There were many fine runners at the ancient Olympics. Some may have run *faster* than the Binkertons. But none ever ran harder.

They ran to the only hiding place they knew.

Joshy? I'm still hungry.

Shhh!

The Binkertons had a problem. They were ready to go home, but they had to stay hidden — and as long as they were hidden, they couldn't finish the Guidebook and go home!

Darn! Too dark to read in here.

Zzzzzz.

The Binkertons waited and waited for a chance to leave. But before they could make a move ... their hiding places began to move.

Uh, oh. What's going on?

Zzzt — snort!

For a long time, the Binkertons rolled around inside their containers. Then, suddenly, the jars began to move in a whole different way.

Psst! Josh! We've stopped rolling. We're rocking now.

Rocking and rolling?

They were on a ship! It was noisy and crowded, and it was moving very quickly.

Why is it so crowded?

I think it's a warship.

WHAT??

Greek Warships

Why not end your visit to ancient Greece with a relaxing cruise on a trireme? A trireme is a warship, but don't be nervous. The Olympic truce is still on, so you'll be perfectly safe. Come aboard!

A trireme is long, light and narrow. It has space (barely) for 170 rowers, jammed in below deck like sardines. They sit in three levels to keep from hitting one another's oars.

A trireme is more than a ship. It's also a weapon. With its jutting point

and sharp blades at the front, it's designed for ramming. It can crash head-on into the side of an enemy ship. It can also be rowed alongside, close enough to slice off the enemy's oars.

Triremes have a huge eye painted on each side to protect the ship against evil, so they're easy to spot. If you see other triremes on your cruise, give them a wave. As long as the Olympic truce is in effect, you're perfectly safe.

Unless, of course, someone *breaks* the truce …

43

AAAGGHH!

EEIIIII!

The Binkertons read as they had never read before. They read so fast, sparks flew off the pages. But the other ship was racing toward them! It was — COMING — THROUGH — THE — SIDE!!! The Binkertons ...

... escaped *just* in the nick of time!

Welcome back!

It was their closest call yet.

You certainly do look rested! Did you have a good time?

Good time? Good time? We've never had a good time. Not once! Not ever!

We didn't mean *those* Olympic Games. We meant — oh, forget it!

The Binkertons vowed right then and there that the only Olympic Games they would watch in future would be on TV.

As they walked out the door of the Good Times Travel Agency, they made a second vow.

But *never*? Well, that's a very long time.

Even for time travelers.

ANCIENT GREECE

Fact or fantasy?

How much can you believe of *Game On in Ancient Greece?*

The Binkerton kids are made up. Their adventures are made up, too. So the story of the Binkertons is just that — a story.

But there really were ancient Greeks, who invented theater and held the first Olympic Games and … well, if you really want to know, read the Guidebook! That's where you'll find the facts. All the information in *Julian T. Pettigrew's Personal Guide to Ancient Greece* is based on historical fact.

Julian T. Pettigrew's Personal Guide to

ANCIENT GREECE

Open this book and your journey's begun. Read every word and your journey is done.

How did a great civilization develop in ancient Greece?

Like many great civilizations, ancient Greece had "roots." Over a thousand years before the Binkertons visited ancient Greece, two earlier civilizations grew up in that part of the world — first the Minoans and later the Mycenaeans.

The Minoans, on the island of Crete, were traders and artists who built magnificent palaces. The Mycenaeans, also traders, were a wealthy, warlike people who lived in heavily fortified towns on the Greek mainland. Stories of the heroes of these civilizations became legends that inspired later Greeks.

After these civilizations collapsed (around 1200 BCE), there was a time of disorder and decline. Then, slowly, scattered communities, separated from one another by mountains and sea, began to form into small city-states. These city-states didn't always have enough farmland for a growing population, so many Greeks went to sea as traders. Trading with other Mediterranean regions made them prosperous. They also picked up interesting new ideas from neighboring cultures. And they began to form new communities in foreign lands.

If you look at the map, you will see the Greek homeland in purple. You will also see, in brown, the colonies that the ancient Greeks formed around the Mediterranean and Black Seas starting in the eighth century BCE.

When did ancient Greece reach its height? What did this civilization achieve?

The Binkertons were lucky enough to experience the very height of ancient Greek civilization — often called the Classical Period. It happened about 2500 years ago (around 500 to 323 BCE). It was a "golden age" of extraordinary new ideas about human beings and the universe, and its center was Athens.

The bold thinkers of classical Greece explored a wide range of ideas. The historian Herodotus wrote what may be the first "history book," a detailed

account of past events in the eastern Mediterranean world, while other ancient Greeks made important contributions to mathematics, biology, astronomy and technology. Greek philosophers came up with questions and ideas that are still studied today, while Greek playwrights wrote plays that are still performed. In art and architecture, ancient Greeks created enduring models of beauty. In medicine, a doctor named Hippocrates taught that disease is the result of natural causes (not the actions of gods) and should be treated by physical means; he is now considered the founder of Western medicine. And of course, the ancient Athenians pioneered a system of government that we now know as democracy — in which citizens had the right to meet and vote to decide matters of importance in their lives.

What do we know about the Olympic Games?

We know quite a lot about the ancient Greeks and their Olympic Games … but not as much as we'd like. The date traditionally given for the first Olympic Games, for example, is 776 BCE. But there's evidence that the Games may have started later than that.

Historians also don't have complete information about the Olympic truce. Although heralds proclaimed it all around the Greek world, it's not clear whether the truce protected all city-states from attack, or only Elis (where Olympia was located).

The order of Olympic events changed through the years, so we are not positive about that, either. And historians don't agree on whether a girl like Emma would have been allowed to watch the Games. (Married women were definitely not allowed.)

One thing we do know — the ancient Olympic Games were not the only religious-and-athletic festival in ancient Greece. In fact, there were four Panhellenic (all-Greece) festivals — the Pythian, Nemean, Isthmian and Olympic Games — each held in a different part of Greece and each honoring a particular god or gods. There were also lots of local festivals held for residents of individual city-states.

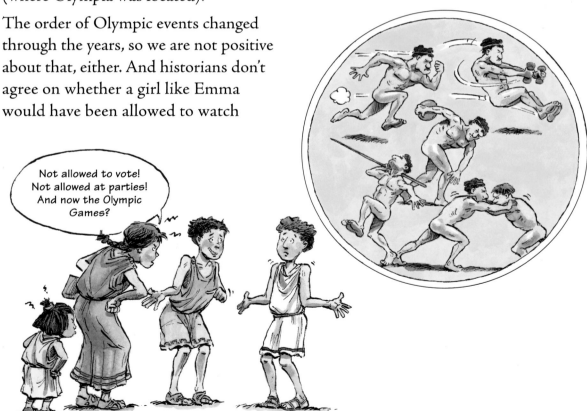

Not allowed to vote! Not allowed at parties! And now the Olympic Games?

How did this civilization end?

The Classical Period of ancient Greece didn't last long — less than 200 years. It ended when the Greek city-states fell under the rule of a northern state called Macedonia. The Macedonian king who completed the conquest, known as Alexander the Great, created a vast empire that extended all the way to Egypt and India. But even though Alexander conquered the Greek city-states, he still felt a deep appreciation for their accomplishments. He admired Greek culture so much, in fact, that he spread it all through his empire.

After Alexander's empire broke up, it was replaced in time by another great power — the Roman Empire. Like Alexander, the Romans also conquered an enormous territory, including Greece. And also like Alexander, they admired the Classical Greeks. They adopted and developed Greek art and culture and spread the Greeks' ideas throughout the Roman empire, which included much of what is now Europe. Eventually, ancient Greece came to be seen as the birthplace of Western civilization.

How do we know about ancient Greece?

We're lucky (and historians are lucky) that the ancient Greeks had a written language that we can still read. Not all the writings of their philosophers, playwrights, historians, poets, etc. were preserved, but we have more from ancient Greece than from many other civilizations.

We are also lucky that the ancient Greeks left behind plenty of objects for us to study. Their art tells wonderful tales of the past — especially their sculptures and the detailed paintings on pottery that show what people did, ate, wore, believed and so on. Plus, some of the magnificent structures designed and built by the Greeks, such as the Parthenon, are still around today to amaze us. Other buildings and objects that became "buried treasure" over the years have been discovered and excavated by archaeologists at sites all over Greece.

And bonus! Because the ancient Greeks were a seafaring people, archaeologists have also been able to find important relics underwater. Ships that sank thousands of years ago on the Aegean Sea are still offering up secrets to archaeologists in diving gear!

Do we know everything about the ancient Greeks? No. Will we learn more in future? Probably. Historians and archaeologists never stop searching for new information about the past. They would love to travel to ancient Greece. If only they could find the right travel agency …

For Further Exploration

Books

Ancient Greece by Peter Ackroyd (Voyages Through Time). DK Publishing, 2005.

Ancient Greece by Peter Benoit (The Ancient World). Children's Press, an imprint of Scholastic Inc., 2013.

Ancient Greece: Archaeology Unlocks the Secrets of Greece's Past by Marni McGee (National Geographic Investigates). National Geographic, 2007.

Eyewitness Ancient Greece by Anne Pearson. DK Publishing, 2014.

Philosophy and Science in Ancient Greece: The Pursuit of Knowledge by Don Nardo. Lucent Books, 2004.

Treasury of Greek Mythology: Classic Stories of Gods, Goddesses, Heroes & Monsters by Donna Jo Napoli. National Geographic Children's Books, 2011.

Websites & DVDs

"Ancient Greece 101," National Geographic, 2018. https://video.nationalgeographic.com/video/101-videos/00000162-b662-d72d-a9fa-b7f367360000

The Greek Guide to Greatness video series, National Geographic Studios, 2016. https://www.pbslearningmedia.org/collection/the-greek-guide-to-greatness/

"This is Sparta," TED-Ed, 2016.
https://ed.ted.com/lessons/this-is-sparta-fierce-warriors-of-the-ancient-world-craig-zimmer

"Welcome to the Ancient Olympic Games," The International Olympic Committee, 2018.
https://www.olympic.org/ancient-olympic-games

Ancient Greece: A Journey Back in Time (Lost Treasures of the Ancient World), Kultur International Films, 2006.

Secrets of the Parthenon, PBS NOVA, WGBH Educational Foundation, 2008.

Historic Sites and Museums

Time travel can be tricky! But if you're lucky, someday you might be able to travel to *modern* Greece, where you can visit the Parthenon and other famous sites, such as the site of the ancient games at Olympia. You might also be able to find museums with ancient Greek collections closer to home.

The Acropolis (and Parthenon), Athens, Greece
http://odysseus.culture.gr/h/3/eh355.jsp?obj_id=2384

The Archaeological Site & Museum of Olympia
http://odysseus.culture.gr/h/3/eh355.jsp?obj_id=2358

The British Museum, London, U.K.
http://www.ancientgreece.co.uk

The Metropolitan Museum of Art, New York, U.S.A.
https://www.metmuseum.org/art/online-features/metkids/videos/MetKids-How-can-I-recognize-ancient-Greek-architecture

National Archaeological Museum, Athens, Greece
http://www.namuseum.gr/en

Index